How to Grow a
DRAGON

Rachel Morrisroe · Steven Lenton

PUFFIN

For Mum and Dad, the world's most magical parents.
I love you x – R. M.

For Lua. Welcome to Planet Earth! Lots of love x – S. L.

PUFFIN BOOKS

UK | USA | Canada | Ireland | Australia | India | New Zealand | South Africa
Puffin Books is part of the Penguin Random House group of companies whose
addresses can be found at global.penguinrandomhouse.com.

www.penguin.co.uk   www.puffin.co.uk   www.ladybird.co.uk

Penguin
Random House
UK

First published 2023
001

Text copyright © Rachel Morrisroe, 2023
Illustrations copyright © Steven Lenton, 2023
The moral right of the author and illustrator has been asserted

Printed in China
ISBN: 978–0–241–39225–6

The authorized representative in the EEA is Penguin Random House Ireland,
Morrison Chambers, 32 Nassau Street, Dublin D02 YH68

A CIP catalogue record for this book is available from the British Library

All correspondence to: Puffin Books, Penguin Random House Children's,
One Embassy Gardens, 8 Viaduct Gardens, London SW11 7BW

Please step inside Mr Pottifer's shop,
where wondrous plants fill the shelves to the top.

Although Mr Pottifer looks quite alarming,
carnivorous plants can be awfully charming.

Here's Sarah, who's brilliant at planting and sowing.
She has quite the talent for magical growing.

And last but not least, please meet sparkly Sprout –
as unicorns go, he's the smartest about.

The friends spend their days potting flowers and trees,
and feeding jam doughnuts to sugar snap peas.

They groom dandelions,

and give dogbane walks.
(Just twice round the block
gives the sturdiest stalks.)

One morning, the postman arrived at the door.
"This letter's been making a terrible roar!"

DRAGODIL
SEEDS

read the spidery writing.

VARIETY PACK

MAY BE PRONE TO IGNITING!

FIRECYNTHS – make quite remarkable guard pets.
(But may make a mess of your living room carpets.)

SKYDRANGEAS – great transport for when you are tired.
(Please carry a sick bag, in case it's required.)

SMOKUSES – helpful for doing the cooking.
(But may eat your laundry up when you're not looking.)

Please plant in a pot, sprinkle spoonfuls of spice,
add three shakes of pepper and clap your hands twice.

Sarah looked worried; her eyes wide as saucers.
"What if they gobble us up in three courses?"

But Pottifer started to
dance in his pot.
"My dear, let's be brave –
we should grow
the whole lot!"

She pulled on her gloves and she reached for the seeds.
They grizzled and growled in a bid to be freed.

She sowed them with chili, then cried out, "Stand back!
The room filled with smoke that was grimy and black.

The soil set alight.
Sarah shouted, "Look out!"
The little pots fizzled
and flamed . . .

. . . then went out.

"I wonder . . ." said Sarah. "These plants are a puzzle!"
Sprout reassured her by giving a nuzzle.

She tried spicy chicken,
and ghost peppers too,

but finally cracked it
with hot vindaloo . . .

She added the pepper,
and sparks started whizzing.
She clapped her hands twice,
and the pots began fizzing!

Smoking spirals of smoke filled the air.

The shop started shaking,

and then came a . . .

BooOOoM!

Soon, **dragons** were squidged in the shop like sardines –
purples and oranges, blues, reds and greens!

Sprout hid his eyes. Mr P said, "Oh crumbs,"
    as they knocked over shelves with their scaly-tailed bums.

They **ROARED** at the beans,
and they sizzled Sprout's tail.
The friends tried to calm them,
to little avail.

Then, one scared the socks off the gardening gnomes.
"I think," Mr P said, "these dragons need homes!"

The flytrap spread news of his clever idea,
"Roll up, roll up. Get your free dragons here!"

Right round the block
formed an orderly queue –
as some left with one dragon.
Some took home two!

But just the next day, all the pets were returned.

"My sofa's all singed,
and my curtains are burned!"

"Mine chased the school bus!"

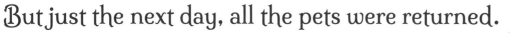

"Well, mine ate my washing!"

"Mine has a bottom that
seems to like squashing!"

"This riding malarkey is NOT easy-peasy.
The wild loop-the-looping makes everyone queasy."

"Well," Mr Pottifer said with a frown,
"as shop-keepers go, I'm the worst one in town!"

Sarah thought hard . . .

. . . then she had an idea.

"I've got it," she shouted. "There's no need to fear!
Perhaps I can train them with something to eat –
I bet they'll behave for the right yummy treat."

She watered some sausage-shaped seeds with hot gravy . . .

and saplings appeared
that were luscious and wavy!

Then, great spicy frankfurters bloomed from the trees
and dangled deliciously, scenting the breeze.

By now, it was chaos. The dragons were swooping,

some sneezing,

some hiccuping,

some loop-the-looping.

They smoked out the village
with spikes all a-bristle . . .

but everything changed with the blast of a whistle.

For Sarah had loaded two open-top wagons
with freshly picked frankfurter treats for the dragons.

"Sit!" she commanded.
"Good dragons – give claw!"

And soon, she had trained them to do every chore!

They heated the burgers
with simmering flickers.

They glided to school,

and did not eat the knickers.

The Firecynths proudly began to stand guard.
(And burned burglars' bums as they ran from the yard!)

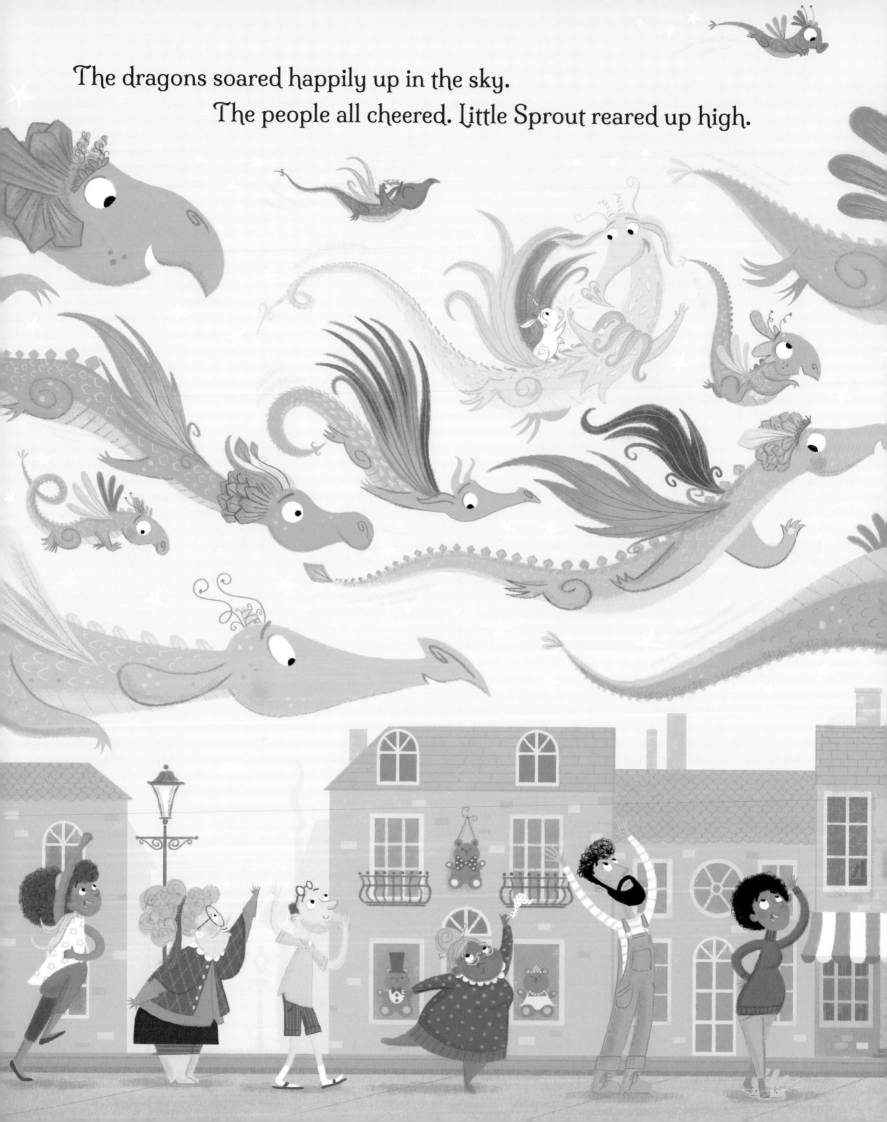

The dragons soared happily up in the sky.
The people all cheered. Little Sprout reared up high.

"Hooray!" said the flytrap. "They're so well behaved!
Oh, Sarah, you've done it! The day has been saved!"

MR POTTIFER'S
PARLOUR OF PLANTS

The next day, the postman arrived by Skydrangea.

"My post round this morning
has NEVER been stranger . . .

This parcel's been making a right royal racket!"
he said, handing Sarah an oyster-shell packet.